the
Crookedtree

jeff s. barganier

To order additional copies of this book, contact:
Xlibris
844-714-8691
www.Xlibris.com
Orders@Xlibris.com

ISBN: Softcover   978-1-4500-4396-0
        Hardcover   978-1-4500-4397-7
        EBook   979-8-3694-0588-8

Library of Congress Control Number: 2010902086

Print information available on the last page

Rev. date: 08/17/2023

One long ago Spring in a great forest, the seed of an ancient hickory tree sprouted by a stream at the bottom of a hill. The large, beautiful trees all around hardly noticed as the little tree poked its head from beneath his winter blanket of brown leaves and straw and peered across the wide forest floor. In his first spring of life even the tiny ferns were taller than the little tree and many tiny, crawly creatures that lived among the tiny ferns would hurry by, mostly ignoring their new little neighbor.

As he grew, all the animals would come to the stream and drink: the deer, bear, possum, wild turkey, squirrels, rabbits, an occasional skunk, slithering snakes, wise owls, feisty bobcats and many colorful birds. Kindly, they were all careful not to step on the little tree and after many seasons he had grown tall and strong. Then tiny ferns rested in the shade of his branches and all the critters of the forest took note of his presence and beauty.

He grew and grew until he could see a good distance through the forest to the top of the hill where he saw a great tree that looked just like him, only much, much larger and very majestic. The old tree at the top of the hill smiled down at his son.

The young tree longed to tear himself from the bottom of the hill and go set his roots down next to the old hickory but this was not possible; so they admired each other from a distance.

During autumn, his father's leaves would ride the wind down the hill. The young tree's leaves would take flight too, and the leaves of the two trees would dance and play together on a joyous journey through the forest to far away places.

Then one day dark clouds encircled the forest and the wind began to blow very hard. The young tree swayed back and forth in the wind, trying with all his might not to break. He tried to be brave for his father who stood firm on the hill, unbending, though the wind struck the mighty old tree with all its fury. The sky became like night and the wind blew harder still. The young tree cried out to his father. But through the darkness, amidst the storm, there was no answer.

Morning came and light filtered through the forest once again. The birds were singing, critters were crawling and the tiny ferns stretched toward the sun. Some squirrels chattered good mornings to each other from distant tree tops. And other animals peeped from their homes in the forest, greeting the day, thankful the storm had passed. But it soon became apparent to all that something was terribly wrong.

The wind had blown the top out of the young tree and torn away some of its branches leaving it leaning into the forest barely alive. He could hardly lift his head to look up the hill toward his father. But when he did he saw the mighty old tree standing atop the hill, majestic as ever, smiling down at him.

When he saw his father standing on the hill in the sunshine smiling down at him, he felt much stronger. He tried to straighten, but no matter how hard he tried, he just couldn't. Part of his roots had come out of the soft wet ground. So he determined to grow just as he stood.

He rested as best he could on the branches of a kind tree nearby, until one day he had grown strong enough to stand alone, though still leaning awkwardly. In fact, because of the way he leaned over, he grew even stronger than before when he was straight like all the other trees.

Seasons passed and after several years the young tree's open wounds healed. He was able to sprout a strong, new limb where his top had broken off and other new limbs grew from his side. He twisted and turned his new branches back toward the stream where the sun could be found. But as he zigzagged back toward the sun, he became more and more crooked until he almost looked like a big Z hanging in the forest.

All the other tall, stately trees reached up to the sky effortlessly. They looked down upon the now crooked tree in their midst and laughed. "He's not one of us," they said. "What value has a crooked tree?" The tiny ferns heard the tall trees laughing and making fun of the crooked tree and grew closer to him so he would not feel alone. They grew so close, in fact, that they soon began to grow right up the crooked tree's back and out onto his twisted branches.

When the crawly creatures that lived among the ferns saw this, they too climbed up upon the crooked tree and lived there among the ferns. When the birds came to catch the crawly creatures, they would sit among the ferns on his crooked branches and sing their most beautiful songs. Then all the creatures of the forest would come to his crooked side, sip life-giving water from the stream and enjoy the beautiful songs.

The crooked tree received so much attention because of his crookedness that the tall, stately trees became very jealous. They tried to block the sun and rain from the crooked tree so he would die. They would sometimes fling their branches down at him but he was so twisted that they often missed. So he twisted on through life as best he could.

He would often look up the hill at his beautiful father and wish to be at his side, away from the cruel trees around him. And he lived for autumn when his father's leaves would ride the wind down the hill and dance with his.

One sunny day two men appeared in the forest. The crooked tree watched as they came closer and closer until, finally, they stopped right under his crooked branches. All the animals hid and watched the men as they stood talking beneath the crooked tree. One man was tall, thin and spoke softly. He wore an old brown hat and chewed on a straw. His face was calm, eyes kind and movements gentle. The other man was short and stocky. He had a thick, dark beard, spoke with a deep voice and had the large, strong hands of a woodsman. In one of his large hands, the short, bearded man carried a large, sharp axe.

When the tall, stately trees saw the woodman's axe they called down to the crooked tree. "There, see that axe," they said. "That axe is for you crooked tree. They've come to cut you down and carry you away so you will not ugly up our forest anymore." Then the birds stopped their singing and the tiny little ferns covered their eyes. Even the little crawly creatures stopped and held their breath as they watched the men below. The crooked tree was very sad and lifted his gloomy eyes to see his father looking down from above.

Then the tall man pointed through the forest toward the top of the hill saying to the woodsman, "I'm going to build a great, white house on that hill by the great hickory. I want you to make me a beautiful road that will enter by this stream and curl through the woods to the top of the hill where my house will be."

"Yes, sir," said the woodsman. "I'll make you a grand road, for sure, I will. Shall I start by cutting down this crooked tree?" he asked.

"Oh! No," said the tall man. "This tree is like no other I have ever seen. The ferns grow on its back, the birds sing beautiful songs from its branches and it shares its life with all who come to it. Its shape is beautiful compared to the common straight trees in the forest. I want my road to wind beneath its branches so that all who come to my house on the hill will enter by way of the crooked tree."

"Fine," the woodsman replied, "I'll cut down these tall, straightly trees and make fire wood of them for the winter. But the crooked tree shall live forever, greeting all who enter by your road."

Hearing this, the crooked tree twisted and stretched its branches toward the blue, cloudless sky. The birds began to sing melodiously, flying off into the forest, spreading the word about the man with the old, brown hat and kind face who was to build a great, white house on the hill. The tiny little ferns clapped their hands. The crawly creatures let out a big breath and raced about their way with great joy. The animals danced and played in the forest. And the majestic, old hickory looked down with great pride and smiled at the crooked tree by the stream at the bottom of the hill.